Big Hippo and Little Hippo

Written by Jill Eggleton
Illustrated by Fraser Williamson

In this book you will see...

The place in the book

Big Hippo and Little Hippo lived in a mud pool.

One day, Big Hippo said to Little Hippo, "**This mud pool is getting** smaller. **There is mud for me, but there is no mud for you. You will have to go.**"

And he pushed Little Hippo.

Little Hippo was **mad**!

"I'm not going," he said.
**"I was here first.
You will have to go!"**

And he pushed Big Hippo.

Little Hippo will...

stay in the mud pool?

go away?

Little Hippo pushed and...

Big Hippo pushed.

They pushed and pushed and **pushed**.
And then Big Hippo
pushed Little Hippo
THWUMMP
out of the mud pool!
What will Little Hippo do?

Little Hippo had to go away
to find a new mud pool.
He walked and walked and walked.
The sun got hotter and hotter and hotter!

“**Mud, mud,**” said Little Hippo.
“**Where is a mud pool?**”

Little Hippo will...

find a mud pool?

not find a mud pool?

Little Hippo sat down on the ground.
He was very hot.
The sun had made big cracks in his back.

"I can't walk," said Little Hippo.
"I'm sick."

And Little Hippo shut his eyes.

Big Hippo sat in the mud pool.
He was hot, too, but
he had mud on his back.
It was cool.
Where is Little Hippo?
What is he doing now?
Big Hippo is...
happy?
sad?

Then Big Hippo saw the animals.
"Little Hippo is sick!
Little Hippo is sick!"
shouted the animals.

Big Hippo jumped
out of the mud pool.
And he ran.
He ran very fast.
He saw Little Hippo on the ground.

"Come back to the mud pool,"
said Big Hippo.
"You can have all the mud.
I'm sorry I made you go."

Little Hippo will...

go back to
the mud pool?

not go back to
the mud pool?

The animals came with leaves.
They put leaves on Little Hippo.

Then they helped him
back to the mud pool.
They put mud on Little Hippo's back.

"I'm not sick now,"
said Little Hippo.

Why is Little Hippo not sick now?

Then it rained.
It rained and **rained**.
The mud pool got bigger and
bigger and **bigger**.

"Look," said Little Hippo
to Big Hippo.
"There's mud for you and
mud for me."
And mud for me!
And mud for me!
And mud for me!
"OK," said Big Hippo.
"We can all have mud!"
The End

Story sequence

Did the story go like this?

Did the story go like this?

3

4

3

4

Word Bank

back 

leaves 

cracks

mud pool 

ground